Bubba and Beau
Meet the Relatives

Kathi Appelt   Arthur Howard

Voyager Books
Harcourt, Inc.

Orlando Austin New York San Diego Toronto London

For Aunt Tootsie, the best aunt in the world—K. A.

www.HarcourtBooks.com

First Voyager Books edition 2008

Voyager Books is a trademark of Harcourt, Inc., registered in the United States of America
and/or other jurisdictions.

The Library of Congress has cataloged the hardcover edition as follows:
Appelt, Kathi, 1954–
Bubba and Beau meet the relatives/Kathi Appelt; illustrated by Arthur Howard.
p. cm.
Summary: While preparing for a visit from some relatives—and even after they arrive—
Bubba and Beau want nothing more than to sink their paws into the squishy, squashy mud hole.
[1. Hospitality—Fiction. 2. Mud—Fiction. 3. Dogs—Fiction.] I. Howard, Arthur, ill. II. Title.
PZ7.A6455Bx 2004
[E]—dc21 2003004983
ISBN 978-0-15-216630-4
ISBN 978-0-15-206136-4 pb

H G F E D C B A

The display type was set in Cloister Oldstyle Bold.
The text type was set in Cloister Oldstyle.
Color separations by Bright Arts Ltd., Hong Kong
Manufactured by South China Printing Company, Ltd., China
Production supervision by Christine Witnik
Designed by Arthur Howard and Judythe Sieck

Chapter One

"The relatives are coming!" cried Mama Pearl.

Suddenly there was *a lot* to do. First Mama Pearl went on a home improvement spree.

Then she handed out orders.

Next came the cooking. Never in all their born days had
Bubba and Beau seen so much stirring and stewing.
Big Bubba even baked his boot-kickin'
Bodacious Banana Buttermilk Pie.

Yep, Bubbaville was abuzz.

Chapter Two

The only place that was safe from all the to-do
was the garden, home of...

the MUD HOLE!

Bubba and Beau loved its squishy squish.
They loved its squashy squash.
Most of all, they loved the way it oozed
between their fingers and toes and paws.
"Wheeeee!" squealed Bubba.
"Arooooo!" bayed Beau.

Sister, that mud hole was
better than pickled eggs.

When Mama Pearl saw Bubba and Beau, she swooned. "But the relatives will be here any minute!" she cried.

"Only one thing to do," said Big Bubba.

Bubba fussed. Beau whined.

Mama Pearl was not deterred.
She dressed Bubba in his brand-new sailor suit.
Bubba hated that sailor suit. It was tight. It was stiff.
It was scratchier than the toilet brush.
Beau got a new bandana. Yuck!

Chapter Three

When the relatives drove up, it was jubilation galore!
First there was Granddaddy Bubba.

Then there was Grandma Ruby.

Next, Aunt Sapphire.

And last, Cousin Arlene and her dog, Bitsy.

Honey, it was froufrou city.

Bubba got passed all around.
Granddaddy Bubba held him
up to the sky. "This is one
fine little Bubba," he said.

Grandma Ruby held him
to her chest.
"He's the best Bubba ever!"
she cried.

Aunt Sapphire planted
her big red lips right
on his cheek.

Cousin Arlene got passed
all around, too.

"Aren't they adorable?" asked Aunt Sapphire.
All the relatives sighed.

Chapter Four

A tour was the next order of business.
Mama Pearl showed the relatives
the sparkly clean house. Big Bubba
showed off Earl, his trusty pickup truck.
Earl's coat shone like a mirror.

Finally, Mama Pearl and Big Bubba showed
the relatives the garden.

Bubba and Beau looked at each other.
They looked at Cousin Arlene and Bitsy.
And then, they headed straight . . .

for the MUD HOLE!!!
Brother, it was paradise found.

"Wheeeee!" squealed Bubba.

"Ooooooh!" squealed Cousin Arlene.

"Arooooo!" bayed Beau.

"Yip! Yip! Yip!" yipped Bitsy.

So long, scratchy sailor suit.
Bye-bye, itchy bandana.
Adios, frilly dress and
froufrou hair bows.

"Only one thing to do," said Big Bubba.

Yeehaw, honey!
It was a picture-perfect
moment in Bubbaville.

Chapter Five

"Supper's on!" said Mama Pearl at last.
First they started chowing down. Then they
started catching up.

Bubba and Beau and Cousin Arlene and Bitsy
had never heard so much yammering. Yes siree,
those relatives caught up till the cows came home.

Afterwards, Big Bubba served up his boot-kickin' Bodacious Banana Buttermilk Pie. Sister, it was better than a trip to Graceland.

Finally, the sun began to set.

Bye-bye, Granddaddy Bubba.
Bye-bye, Grandma Ruby.
Bye-bye, Aunt Sapphire.
Bye-bye, Cousin Arlene and Bitsy.

Y'all come back now, ya hear?